INTERGALACTIC JUNKYARD

By
Ryan Michael Upton

Table of Contents

COPYRIGHT PAGE ... 6

Before The Adventure Begins ... 7

CHAPTER 1 ... 9

The Dinner Disaster ... 9

CHAPTER 2 ... 13

Meet the Crew ... 13

CHAPTER 3 ... 17

The Workshop ... 17

CHAPTER 4 ... 21

The Last Rider ... 21

CHAPTER 5 ... 25

The Take Off ... 25

CHAPTER 6 ... 30

In Orbit ... 30

CHAPTER 7 ... 35

De Orbit ... 35

CHAPTER 8 ... 43

On the surface ... 43

CHAPTER 9 ... 53

The standoff ... 53

CHAPTER 10 ... 56

The First Strike ... 56

CHAPTER 11 ... 59

The Junkyard Manager..59
CHAPTER 12 67
Outside..67
CHAPTER 13 72
The Junkyard..72
CHAPTER 14 77
Meeting Gavin..77
CHAPTER 15 81
The request for help..81
CHAPTER 16 84
Helping 84
CHAPTER 17 88
The Good Deal..88
CHAPTER 18 97
The Strange House 97
CHAPTER 19 101
The Junkyard Manager..101
CHAPTER 20 107
Treasure in the Dirt 107
CHAPTER 21 112
Repairs 112
CHAPTER 22 117
The Mud Field 117
CHAPTER 23 122

Incoming..122
CHAPTER 24 125
The Sky Breaks 125
CHAPTER 25 128
The Fire Cloud 128
CHAPTER 26 132
Clean Up..132
CHAPTER 27 137
Something Big 138
CHAPTER 28 142
The Giant Floozag...142
CHAPTER 29 146
Hello, Big Floozag 146
CHAPTER 30 148
The Keeper 149
CHAPTER 31 151
Old Promises 151
CHAPTER 32 155
The Floozag's Choice 155
CHAPTER 33 160
Awakening the Machine 160
CHAPTER 34 163
Follow that Maintenance Robot 163
CHAPTER 35 167

Away they go..167
CHAPTER 36 171
The Hammerhead 171
CHAPTER 37 177
It is Working..177
CHAPTER 38 181
A New Beginning..181

COPYRIGHT PAGE

INTERGALACTIC JUNKYARD

ISBN 978-1-7645764-7-5 (paperback)

First published in Australia in 2026.

Kindle Edition.

Cover design and illustrations by the author.

Before The Adventure Begins

Space is full of amazing things: shining stars, mysterious planets, and incredible spaceships. But have you ever wondered what happens to those spaceships when they grow old, break down, or can no longer fly?

Somewhere far beyond Earth, there is a place called the **Intergalactic Junkyard**.

It isn't an ordinary junkyard.

It's a gigantic drifting collection of retired rockets, strange alien machines, forgotten gadgets, and mysterious pieces of technology from all across the universe.

When Jacob, Sybil, and Mathew learn that their Uncle Ryan is taking them there, they can hardly believe it. What begins as a normal evening quickly turns into an unforgettable adventure among towering piles of cosmic scrap, curious discoveries, and surprising creatures hiding inside ancient spacecraft.

But the Intergalactic Junkyard isn't just a pile of space junk…

It's a place filled with mysteries, strange machines, and secrets waiting to be uncovered.

So get ready to explore, imagine, and blast off on an exciting journey to the most unusual junkyard in the entire galaxy.

CHAPTER 1

The Dinner Disaster

Jacob stared suspiciously at the plate in front of him.

Something green slowly slid across the mashed potatoes.

Something orange wobbled beside it.

Jacob poked the food with his fork.

The green thing wiggled.

Jacob leaned closer and squinted.

"Is it… moving?" he whispered.

Across the table, Sybil calmly ate her dinner without even looking up.

Mathew swung his legs under his chair and hummed happily, as if dinner were the best part of the day.

But Jacob's face twisted into pure disgust.

"YUCK!"

Before anyone could stop him, Jacob grabbed the plate and flung the food across the table.

Vegetables splattered everywhere.

A piece of broccoli bounced off the wall.

A carrot slowly slid down the refrigerator door.

The room went completely silent.

Then…

“JACOB!”

Uncle Ryan jumped up so quickly his chair scraped loudly across the floor.

He pushed his round yellow glasses up his nose and pointed a finger straight at Jacob.

“Don’t throw your food!”

Jacob shrank in his chair.

“But it’s disgusting,” he muttered.

Uncle Ryan folded his arms.

“That’s not the point,” he said firmly.
“You still don’t throw food across the table.”

Jacob looked down.

“I’m sorry.”

For a moment, Uncle Ryan looked very serious.

Then suddenly…

He smiled.

“Well,” Uncle Ryan said, adjusting his lab coat,
“You might want to eat something first.”

CHAPTER 2

Meet the Crew

Uncle Ryan pushed his round yellow glasses up his nose and smiled.

"Since we're about to go on a very unusual trip," he said, "I suppose it's only fair that everyone properly meets the crew."

Jacob groaned softly.

"Do we really need introductions?"

He was already examining a strange tool sitting on Uncle Ryan's worktable, turning it over in his hands.

Jacob loved machines.
Engines.
Buttons.
Levers.

If it whirred, sparked, or exploded, Jacob was interested.

Sybil leaned over his shoulder.

"Maybe don't press anything yet," she said calmly. "We don't know what it does."

Jacob grinned.

“That’s the fun part.”

Sybil shook her head but smiled.

She loved solving puzzles and figuring things out. If something strange was happening, Sybil usually noticed it before anyone else.

Behind them, Mathew bounced excitedly from foot to foot.

“So… when do we leave Earth?” he asked.

Uncle Ryan chuckled.

Mathew loved everything.

Robots.
Aliens.
Spaceships.

And especially adventures.

“Patience,” Uncle Ryan said.

Mathew leaned closer.

“But are we really going to space?”

Uncle Ryan lowered his voice like he was about to reveal the greatest secret in the universe.

"Yes."

The room went very quiet.

Jacob stopped fiddling with the tool.

Sybil leaned forward.

Mathew froze mid-bounce.

"For where?" Jacob asked.

Uncle Ryan smiled slowly.

"To the place where old spaceships go when they retire."

Mathew's mouth dropped open.

"Wait… you mean like a junkyard?"

Uncle Ryan nodded.

"But not just any junkyard."

He spread his arms wide.

"The biggest spaceship junkyard in the entire galaxy."

Sybil's eyes widened.

"A whole graveyard of spacecraft?" she said thoughtfully.

"Exactly."

Jacob's serious expression suddenly changed into a grin.

"Do they still have engines?"

"Some do," Uncle Ryan said.

Jacob's grin grew wider.

Mathew could barely stand still.

"It's called…" Uncle Ryan said, pausing dramatically.

"The Intergalactic Junkyard."

Mathew jumped.

"WE'RE GOING TO SPACE?!"

Uncle Ryan laughed.

"Adventure starts early."

And the three children suddenly realized that tonight would be very different from an ordinary visit to their uncle.

CHAPTER 3

The Workshop

The children followed Uncle Ryan down a narrow metal walkway.

The air smelled faintly like oil and warm metal.

Below them, a huge room stretched, packed with machines.

Wires hung from the ceiling like tangled vines.

Lights blinked across glowing control panels.

Strange humming and buzzing sounds echoed through the workshop.

Mathew spun in a slow circle, staring at everything.

"Whoa… what is this place?"

Uncle Ryan spread his arms proudly.

"This," he said, "is my workshop."

Jacob's eyes immediately locked onto a half-built engine sitting on a nearby table.

He stepped closer, studying the gears and wires.

"Is that a plasma engine?" he asked.

Uncle Ryan smiled.

"Very good. Most people would think it's just a pile of scrap."

Sybil wandered toward a large control panel covered in glowing buttons and strange symbols.

She tilted her head, studying the screen.

"Are these star maps?" she asked.

Uncle Ryan nodded.

"Charts for hundreds of systems."

Mathew, meanwhile, had discovered a robotic arm hanging from the ceiling.

It slowly rotated and beeped.

Mathew waved at it.

"Hello, robot!"

The arm beeped again.

Mathew grinned.

"I think it likes me."

Uncle Ryan chuckled.

“Careful. That one assembles rocket engines.”

At the far end of the workshop stood a massive metal door.

It was taller than a house.

Mathew pointed.

“What’s behind that?”

Uncle Ryan’s smile grew wider.

“That,” he said, “is the really exciting part.”

The children hurried after him as he walked to the door.

He pressed a glowing button on the wall.

For a moment, nothing happened.

Then…..

WHOOOOSH

The giant door slowly slid open.

Bright white light poured into the workshop.

The children shielded their eyes.

And then they saw it.

A sleek red spaceship sat inside the hangar beyond the door.

Its metal surface gleamed under bright lights.

Small blue lights blinked along its wings.

Jacob's jaw dropped.

Sybil stared in amazement.

Mathew began jumping up and down.

"A SPACESHIP!"

Uncle Ryan folded his arms proudly.

"Kids," he said,

"Meet the ship that's taking us to the **Intergalactic Junkyard**."

CHAPTER 4

The Last Rider

Uncle Ryan led the children across the busy workshop floor.

Machines hummed softly around them.

Lights blinked on control panels.

At the far end of the room sat something bright red.

Mathew's mouth fell open.

"Whoa…"

In the middle of the workshop, a sleek red spacecraft rested.

It was shaped a little like a car.

But longer.

Smoother.

And definitely built for space.

Bright metal wings curved along its sides.

Small blue lights blinked along the edges.

Painted across the side in bold silver letters were the words:

LAST RIDER

Sybil stepped closer and gently ran her hand along the smooth metal surface.

“Is this… your spaceship?” she asked.

Uncle Ryan nodded proudly.

“Sure is.”

Jacob circled the ship slowly, studying every detail.

He crouched near the engine vents.

“Those are plasma thrusters,” he said, impressed. “You built this yourself?”

“Every bolt,” Uncle Ryan replied.

Jacob tried to lean casually against the ship, pretending not to be amazed.

But the excitement in his eyes gave him away.

“What can it do?” he asked.

Uncle Ryan grinned.

“Well…”

He tapped the side of the ship.

“It can fly faster than sound.”

Mathew’s eyes widened.

“Faster than rockets?”

“Much faster.”

Uncle Ryan leaned closer and lowered his voice dramatically.

“And if everything works properly…”

He tapped the hull again.

“…it can take us all the way to the **Intergalactic Junkyard**.”

Mathew jumped up and down.

“Can we ride in it?!”

Uncle Ryan laughed.

“That’s exactly the plan.”

Behind them, the engines at the back of the ship suddenly began to glow.

Soft blue light filled the workshop.

The ship hummed quietly.

Jacob looked up.

Sybil smiled.

Mathew bounced with excitement.

Uncle Ryan walked toward the hatch and pressed a button.

The door slowly opened.

“Well then,” he said.

“Everyone aboard.”

The adventure was about to begin.

CHAPTER 5

The Take Off

Far away from busy cities…
Far away from crowded spaceports…

Uncle Ryan's workshop was hidden in a very unusual place.

High on a rocky cliff beside the roaring ocean stood an old stone castle.

From the outside, it looked like something from a fairy tale.

Tall towers stretched into the cloudy sky.

Warm lights glowed from the windows.

Waves crashed against the rocks far below.

A narrow stone path wound its way up to the front gate.

But the castle held a secret.

Hidden deep inside the cliffs beneath it was a massive metal doorway.

Behind that doorway was Uncle Ryan's workshop.

And inside that workshop…

A bright red spaceship called **The Last Rider**.

Very soon, that spaceship would blast into the sky.

Carrying Uncle Ryan, Jacob, Sybil, and Mathew on the greatest adventure of their lives.

Storm clouds rolled across the sky as waves crashed against the cliffs.

Rain tapped against the castle towers.

Far below the stone walls, inside the hidden launch hangar, bright lights illuminated the enormous chamber.

The hangar doors slowly began to open.

Wind and rain rushed through the tunnel beneath the castle.

Inside the Last Rider, the engines hummed louder and louder.

Blue flames flickered at the back of the ship.

Uncle Ryan sat in the pilot's chair and adjusted the controls.

"Everyone buckled in?" he asked.

Jacob tightened his seat belt.

“Ready.”

Sybil checked the glowing screens beside her.

“All systems look stable,” she said.

Mathew pressed his face against the window.

“I can see the ocean!”

Uncle Ryan smiled.

“Good.”

He flipped a switch.

The engines roared.

“Launching in three…”

Mathew grabbed the armrests.

“Two…”

Jacob leaned forward, watching the controls.

“ONE!”

BOOOOM!

The Last Rider blasted upward from the hidden hangar.

The ship shot out from the cliffs and straight into the stormy sky.

Four bright blue engines flared behind it, leaving glowing trails through the clouds.

Inside the cockpit, Uncle Ryan held the controls steady.

“Climbing through the atmosphere,” he said calmly.

Jacob watched the clouds racing past the window.

“We’re going really fast.”

Mathew laughed.

“This is AWESOME!”

Sybil looked upward as the dark storm clouds began to thin.

Then suddenly…..

The ship burst out of the top of the storm.

Above them, the sky was deep black and filled with stars.

Below them, Earth curved gently like a giant blue marble.

Mathew gasped.

"Whoa…"

"We're really in space."

Uncle Ryan smiled as the stars reflected across the cockpit window.

"Next stop…"

He pointed toward the endless field of stars ahead.

"…the **Intergalactic Junkyard**."

CHAPTER 6

In Orbit

The **Last Rider** glided silently through space.

Behind them, the blue curve of Earth slowly drifted farther away.

From up here, the planet looked like a glowing marble floating in darkness.

White clouds curled across its surface like giant spirals.

Mathew pressed his face against the window.

"Wow… Earth looks tiny from up here!"

Sybil leaned closer beside him, studying the stars.

Thousands of tiny lights sparkled across the endless black sky.

"So many stars," she whispered.

Jacob tried to look calm in the pilot's seat.

But even he couldn't stop staring.

Space stretched forever in every direction.

Uncle Ryan adjusted the glowing controls on the dashboard.

The engines hummed softly behind them.

“We’re leaving Earth’s orbit now,” he said.

Mathew turned around.

“Are we going really far?”

Uncle Ryan smiled.

“Oh yes,” he said.

“Very far.”

He tapped a glowing button on the control panel.

A bright star map appeared above the dashboard.

Lines stretched across the galaxy like glowing roads.

One blinking dot marked their destination.

“And we’ll be there sooner than you think.”

Jacob gripped the controls carefully.

“Am I really flying this?” he asked.

Uncle Ryan chuckled.

"Well, I'm helping," he said.
"But you're doing great."

Jacob tried not to grin too much.

Sybil watched the stars slowly drifting past the window.

"So this is what space really looks like," she said quietly.

Then suddenly…..

Mathew pointed excitedly.

"LOOK!"

Everyone turned toward the front window.

At first, it looked like a strange cloud floating among the stars.

But as the **Last Rider** moved closer, the shapes became clearer.

Huge dark silhouettes drifted through space.

Broken ships.

Bent wings.

Giant engines.

Ancient spacecraft floating silently in every direction.

Some ships were enormous.

Others were tiny.

Pieces of metal drifted like glittering space debris.

Lights flickered faintly from forgotten machines.

Mathew's eyes grew huge.

"Whoa…"

Sybil stared in amazement.

"It's like a giant graveyard for spaceships."

Jacob leaned forward in his seat.

"But some of them still look like they work…"

Uncle Ryan smiled.

"Well, kids," he said,

"I think we're almost there."

Ahead of them stretched the most unusual place in the entire galaxy.

Towering mountains of broken spacecraft.

Fields of floating metal.

And secrets hidden among the drifting wreckage.

The **Intergalactic Junkyard**.

CHAPTER 7

De Orbit

Suddenly, a blinking light appeared on the radar screen.

Uncle Ryan noticed it immediately.

"Hmmm…"

Jacob leaned forward.

"What is it?"

Uncle Ryan adjusted the scanner.

"Looks like we're approaching something."

Sybil's eyes widened.

"The junkyard?"

Uncle Ryan smiled.

"Yep."

Outside the window, something enormous slowly began to appear in the darkness of space.

Mathew whispered in awe.

"Whoa…"

Uncle Ryan kept his eyes on the navigation screen while the **Last Rider** glided smoothly through space.

"I mainly fix things," he explained.
"I find broken ships at the junkyard, repair what I can, and sell the working parts. My friend **Gavin** owns the place."

Mathew leaned forward.

"A spaceship cemetery?" he asked.

Uncle Ryan nodded.

"Exactly. When ships get too old, damaged, or unsafe, they're sent there. Some are taken apart for parts. Others float there forever."

Jacob stared out the window thoughtfully.

"So there are thousands of ships out there?"

"Millions," Uncle Ryan said.

Sybil turned toward him.

"Doesn't it get scary?"

Uncle Ryan smiled slightly.

"Sometimes."

Mathew's eyes widened.

"Why?"

Uncle Ryan tapped the radar screen.

"Well, sometimes we find ships that no one remembers sending there."

Jacob frowned.

"What do you mean?"

Uncle Ryan leaned back in his seat.

"Ships that appear out of nowhere. No records. No crew. No explanation."

Sybil looked out at the dark space ahead.

"Ghost ships?"

Uncle Ryan chuckled.

"Some people call them that."

Just then, a faint signal blinked on the scanner.

Beep… Beep…

Jacob noticed it first.

"Uh… Uncle Ryan?"

Ryan leaned forward and squinted at the display.

"That's strange…"

Mathew swallowed.

"What is it?"

Ryan slowly turned the ship toward the signal.

"It looks like," he said quietly,

"…we might be about to find one."

Suddenly, a bright flash lit up the cockpit.

BOOM!

A massive explosion erupted in space ahead of them.

Mathew jumped in his seat.

"Whoa! What was that?!"

Sybil leaned forward, staring out the window.

"Are those… spaceships fighting?"

Jacob's eyes widened.

"That's a battle!"

Uncle Ryan quickly grabbed the controls.

"No, not a battle."

He flipped a switch, and the **Last Rider's** engines shifted into a lower, quieter hum.

"We're getting too close," he said calmly.

Mathew pointed nervously.

"Are they going to shoot us?"

Uncle Ryan shook his head.

"They probably don't even know we're here."

Another explosion flashed across the stars.

Sybil gasped.

"Why are they fighting?"

Ryan frowned as he studied the radar screen.

"No, not fighting," he said.

"It looks like an old ship is about to be retired…"

He gently turned the **Last Rider** away from the explosions.

"…it just created a lot of new junk for the junkyard."

Jacob looked back at the burning debris drifting through space.

"So tomorrow…"

"…you'll be fixing those ships?"

Uncle Ryan smiled slightly.

"Maybe."

Then he pointed ahead into the darkness.

"Because right now…"

"…we've got a junkyard to reach."

The children watched the burning spaceship streak across the sky.

It glowed bright orange as it plunged toward the planet below.

Long trails of fire followed behind it.

Mathew pressed his hands against the window.

"Wow…"

Sybil's eyes sparkled.

"Amazing."

Uncle Ryan nodded.

"When spaceships are too old to fly safely anymore," he explained, "they're brought to this planet."

Jacob leaned forward.

"And then they crash them?"

Uncle Ryan laughed.

"Not exactly."

He pointed toward the atmosphere below.

"The pilots guide them down carefully. When they reach the right point, they deorbit the ship so it lands safely at the junkyard."

Outside the window, the fiery ship grew smaller as it descended.

Mathew watched it disappear into the clouds.

"So the junkyard is on that planet?"

"Yep," Uncle Ryan said.

"A whole world filled with retired spaceships."

Sybil smiled.

“That sounds incredible.”

Jacob folded his arms again, but this time he looked impressed.

“So basically…”

“…it’s the biggest garage in the universe.”

Uncle Ryan grinned.

“That’s one way to describe it.”

He gently pushed the controls forward.

The **Last Rider** began descending toward the glowing planet below.

“Alright, crew,” Uncle Ryan said.

“Let’s go to work.”

CHAPTER 8

On the Surface

The **Last Rider** roared through the upper atmosphere of the planet.

White clouds rushed past the windows as the ship descended smoothly.

Inside the cockpit, the instruments blinked and hummed.

Mathew bounced slightly in his seat.

"We're going into the clouds!"

Sybil leaned closer to the window.

"I can't see the ground yet."

Jacob gripped the armrest as the ship tilted downward.

"Are you sure this thing lands safely?" he asked.

Uncle Ryan smiled calmly and adjusted the controls.

"Relax. The Last Rider has landed thousands of times."

The engines softened to a steady hum.

Below them, the clouds slowly began to thin.

Mathew squinted.

“Hey… I think I see something!”

Sybil leaned forward.

“Is that… metal?”

Uncle Ryan nodded.

“Yep.”

The last layer of cloud drifted away.

Below them, an enormous valley stretched, filled with shapes.

Gigantic shapes.

Broken starships.

Old cruisers.

Massive engines.

Wings, hulls, towers of metal stacked across the landscape.

Jacob’s eyes widened.

"No way…"

Mathew gasped.

"It's huge!"

Uncle Ryan grinned as he guided the ship lower.

"Kids."

"Welcome to the **Intergalactic Junkyard**."

The **Last Rider** settled gently onto the ground.

They all looked out of the windows.

Dust swirled around the landing gear as the engines powered down.

Everywhere they turned, there were piles of old machines.

Broken vehicles.

Rusty metal.

Giant heaps of parts stacked higher than buildings.

Mathew's mouth dropped open.

"Whoa…"

Sybil looked across the enormous yard.

“It’s like a mountain of junk!”

Jacob looked at a rusty piece of metal on the ground.

“So this is the junkyard?”

Uncle Ryan nodded.

“Yep. Ships, vehicles, engines, robots… if it’s broken, it eventually ends up here.”

In the distance, a large crane lifted a wrecked vehicle and dropped it onto a pile with a loud **CRASH**.

Mathew pointed.

“Look at that machine!”

A robot slowly crawled across the ground, sorting through pieces of metal.

“Some of the robots help us sort the parts,” Uncle Ryan explained.

Sybil looked around curiously.

“So, where do you fix the spaceships?”

Uncle Ryan smiled and pointed toward a large metal building at the far end of the yard.

“That’s the workshop.”

Jacob cracked a small smile.

“Finally. Something interesting.”

Uncle Ryan laughed.

“Oh, trust me, you haven’t seen the interesting part yet.”

The children stared through the front window of the **Last Rider**.

Outside, machines moved slowly across the giant junkyard.

A huge crane lifted an old vehicle high into the air and dropped it onto a pile of metal with a loud **CLANG**.

Mathew pointed excitedly.

“Look! It’s picking up the cars!”

Sybil watched the massive piles of scrap stretching across the valley.

“There’s so much stuff here!”

Jacob folded his arms and looked unimpressed.

“So… you basically work in a giant garbage dump.”

Uncle Ryan laughed.

"It might look like junk," he said, "but a lot of these parts are still useful."

He tapped a control panel.

"Engines, computers, navigation systems… sometimes we find parts that are worth a fortune."

Mathew's eyes widened.

"Treasure?"

"Exactly," Uncle Ryan said with a grin.

Just then, a loud **CRASH** echoed across the yard as another vehicle landed on a pile.

Sybil looked toward the far side of the junkyard.

Uncle Ryan nodded.

"That's where the real work happens."

Jacob leaned forward slightly.

"So what's the first thing we're going to fix?"

Uncle Ryan smiled mysteriously.

"He pointed toward the back of the junkyard.

"…there's one ship I've been saving for a special project."

Mathew leaned forward eagerly.

"What kind of ship?"

Uncle Ryan winked.

"One that might still have a few **surprises** left inside."

Inside the workshop, Uncle Ryan switched on a large holographic display.

A glowing blue figure appeared in the air above the workbench.

Mathew's jaw dropped.

"Whoa… is that a robot?"

Sybil leaned closer to the floating blueprint.

The hologram slowly rotated, showing every part of the machine.

Lights blinked along its arms and legs.

Jacob squinted at the labels.

"Communication antenna… damaged optics… exposed cables…"

Uncle Ryan nodded.

“This is the robot I told you about.”

Mathew pointed at the screen.

“That’s what was inside the wrecked ship?”

“Yep,” Uncle Ryan said.

“It’s an advanced service android. Model name: Anistatica.”

Sybil studied the diagram.

“It looks pretty broken.”

Uncle Ryan smiled.

“That’s why it ended up in the junkyard.”

Jacob tilted his head.

“So you’re going to fix it?”

Ryan folded his arms.

“Maybe. If she asks me?”

Mathew’s eyes sparkled.

“What does it do?”

Uncle Ryan tapped a control, and new information appeared on the hologram.

“It was designed to repair ships, analyze systems, and help engineers.”

Jacob raised an eyebrow.

“So basically… it does your job.”

Uncle Ryan laughed.

“Not quite.”

He looked at the damaged sections glowing on the display.

“But if we can get it running again…”

“…it might help us out in the junkyard.”

The hologram flickered slightly.

For a moment, one of the android’s optic sensors flashed.

Sybil noticed it first.

“Uh… Uncle Ryan?”

Ryan looked up.

“Yes?”

Sybil pointed nervously at the hologram.

"I think…"

"…it just moved."

CHAPTER 9

The Standoff

The children stared through the cockpit window.

Two robots stood in the middle of the junkyard.

Neither one moved.

The first robot was enormous. Thick plates of metal covered its body like armor. Heavy pistons and gears formed its powerful arms.

The second robot looked completely different.

Its body shimmered like liquid silver.

Millions of tiny machines flowed across its surface, constantly shifting shape.

Mathew whispered,
"Are they fighting?"

Uncle Ryan leaned forward, studying them carefully.

"Not yet."

Jacob frowned.

"They look frozen."

"They're thinking," Ryan explained.

Both machines were calculating.

Waiting.

Planning.

The heavy metal robot stomped one foot forward.

CLANG.

Across from it, the silver robot's body rippled as its Nanobots rearranged themselves.

Sybil gripped the edge of her seat.

"That one is changing shape."

Ryan nodded slowly.

"The Nanobots are adapting."

Mathew gulped.

"So… who wins?"

Ryan leaned back.

"That depends on who makes the first mistake."

Outside the ship, sparks crackled across the junkyard.

The battle was about to begin.

CHAPTER 10

The First Strike

The air across the junkyard crackled with electricity.

The heavy robot moved first.

With a thunderous step, it lunged forward.

THUD.

The ground shook beneath its weight.

The Nanobot robot reacted instantly.

Its arm flowed like liquid metal, reshaping into a long blade.

CLANG!

Metal struck metal.

The impact echoed across the entire valley.

Inside the ship, Matthew shouted,

"Whoa!"

The heavy robot swung its massive arm again.

But the Nanobot machine dissolved into a cloud of tiny silver particles.

The metal fist smashed straight through empty air.

Sybil gasped.

“It broke apart!”

Ryan shook his head.

“No.”

The swarm reassembled behind the giant robot.

Millions of tiny machines rushed toward the armor plates.

Jacob’s eyes widened.

“It’s trying to get inside!”

The heavy robot spun around, shaking violently.

Orange sparks burst from its joints.

For a moment, the junkyard looked like a storm of blue and orange lightning.

And then,

A voice shouted across the valley.

"Oi! Break it up!"

CHAPTER 11

The Junkyard Manager

The two robots crackled with energy, ready to strike.

Then,

Jacob blinked.

“Wait… what’s that?”

From the far side of the junkyard, a lone figure slowly walked into the open clearing.

An older man.

He wore patched clothes and walked with a long wooden staff. His beard was grey and wild, and his sandals scraped quietly across the dusty ground.

In one hand, he held a small device, turning it slowly as if examining it.

Inside the cockpit, the children stared in disbelief.

Mathew whispered, “Is he… walking toward them?”

Sybil gasped.

"He can't do that!"

Outside, the older man continued forward, completely calm.

The orange sparks from the metal robot lit the ground around him.

The blue glow from the Nanobot machine flickered across his worn clothes.

Jacob looked at Uncle Ryan.

"Does he know those robots are about to fight?"

Ryan frowned, studying the scene carefully.

"I… don't know."

The older man stopped next to the two machines.

The robots still roared with energy, their fists clenched and glowing.

Yet the older man simply leaned on his staff and looked up at them.

Mathew whispered nervously,

"Uh… Uncle Ryan?"

Ryan nodded slowly.

"Yes… I see him."

Sybil's voice was barely audible.

"Why isn't he scared?"

The robots froze for a moment.

And the entire junkyard suddenly went quiet.

Inside the cockpit, Uncle Ryan smiled, "Ahh," Ryan said calmly. "Here comes **Gavin**, the Junkyard Manager."

The children leaned forward to watch.

Jacob frowned. "He doesn't look like a manager."

Ryan chuckled. "Gavin runs this entire place. Nothing moves in the junkyard without him knowing about it."

The two robots continued crackling with orange and blue energy, still facing each other.

Sybil whispered, "What's he doing?"

Mathew's eyes widened. "So he can stop them?"

"Exactly," Ryan said. "Watch."

A faint pulse of light spread out across the junkyard.

The orange robot suddenly stiffened.

The blue Nanobot robot flickered and slowed.

Both machines lowered their arms.

The electricity around them began to fade.

Jacob blinked in surprise.

“He just… turned them off!”

Ryan nodded.

“Not off exactly. More like… telling them the fight is over.”

The junkyard became momentarily quiet again.

Mathew grinned.

“Is Gavin really doing it? Shooing off the troublemakers?”

Ryan laughed softly.

“Yep. Around here, Gavin keeps the peace.”

Then he added with a wink:

“And you’ll want him on your side if you ever get lost in this junkyard.”

Out in the junkyard, the two robots had circled around and were just about to attack each other again.

Orange sparks flew from the heavy metal robot as it leaned forward.

Blue lightning danced across the Nanobot machine as it prepared to strike.

Then,

Tap. Tap. Tap.

Gavin walked straight between them.

He raised his stick and pointed it at the robots.

“Oi! Shoo! Off with ya!” he shouted.
“Go rust somewhere else!”

The robots froze.

Their glowing eyes flickered.

The metal robot made a confused **BZTT…** sound.

The Nanobot robot’s energy dimmed, and it stepped backward.

Gavin waved his stick again like he was chasing away stray animals.

"Move along now!"

Slowly, both robots backed away from each other.

The orange sparks faded.

The blue glow softened.

After a moment, the two ancient machines turned and stomped off in opposite directions across the junkyard.

Gavin shook his head and muttered to himself.

"Ancient war machines…"

He tapped his stick on the ground.

"…can't even handle a walking stick."

Back in the spaceship cockpit, the children burst out laughing.

Mathew wiped tears from his eyes.

"He scared them away!"

Sybil giggled.

"He just told them to go away!"

Jacob shook his head in amazement.

“That was the strangest thing I’ve ever seen.”

Uncle Ryan smiled.

He looked out at the quiet junkyard.

Mathew leaned back in his seat, still giggling.

“I can’t believe it! Two giant war robots… and Gavin just chased them away with a stick!”

Sybil wiped a tear from her eye from laughing.

“That was the funniest thing I’ve ever seen!”

Even Jacob, who usually tried to look serious, was smiling.

“I thought we were about to see a huge battle.”

Uncle Ryan chuckled and leaned back in his chair.

“Sometimes,” he said, “the simplest solution works the best.”

The giant piles of scrap metal sat quietly under the cloudy sky. An old excavator slowly lifted another rusted car and dropped it onto the scrap pile with a loud **CLANG**.

Mathew looked out at the peaceful scene.

“So… what do we do now?”

Uncle Ryan grinned.

"Well," he said, reaching for the controls, "now that the troublemakers are gone…"

"…we can finally go meet Gavin."

Sybil's eyes lit up.

"The junkyard manager?"

Ryan nodded.

"He's the one who helps me find the best broken machines to fix."

Jacob leaned forward.

"Do you think he'll show us something cool?"

Ryan smiled.

"In a place like this?"

He tapped a button on the console.

"There's always something interesting to discover."

CHAPTER 12

Outside

Outside the ship, the junkyard was quiet again.

The wind moved slowly through the piles of scrap metal. Rusty buses, broken machines, and mountains of old parts stretched out in every direction.

But the two ancient robots had not gone far.

The heavy-metal robot stood near an old, rusted bus, its orange glow now faint.

Across the clearing, the Nanobot robot stood beside the excavator, its blue shimmer slowly fading.

Neither one moved.

Inside the cockpit, Uncle Ryan looked out the window and raised an eyebrow.

"Well now," he said.

Jacob leaned forward.

"They didn't leave."

Mathew tilted his head.

"They're just… standing there."

Sybil looked worried.

"Are they going to start fighting again?"

Ryan watched carefully.

"I don't think so."

Outside, the two machines stood silently across the junkyard, as if waiting.

Waiting for something.

Or someone.

Ryan smiled slightly.

"Looks like Gavin told them to cool off."

Jacob crossed his arms.

"So now what are they doing?"

Ryan pointed out the window.

"Thinking."

Mathew blinked.

"Robots think?"

Ryan nodded.

"The old ones do."

Outside, the two ancient machines remained motionless in the quiet junkyard.

Gavin was still watching.

Inside the cockpit, Uncle Ryan pointed toward the junkyard.

"Let's go talk to Gavin."

Mathew jumped up in his seat.

"Really? We get to meet him?"

Ryan nodded.

"If anyone knows what interesting machines are hiding in this junkyard, it's Gavin."

Sybil smiled excitedly.

"I want to see his control device!"

Jacob folded his arms but looked curious.

"I want to know how he stopped those robots."

Outside the window, the junkyard stretched out in every direction—mountains of scrap, rusted vehicles, and old machines waiting to be discovered.

Ryan stood and reached for the hatch controls.

“Well,” he said, “let’s not keep him waiting.”

With a soft **WHIRR**, the spaceship hatch opened.

A metal ramp slowly lowered to the dusty ground below.

The wind carried the smell of rust and oil into the ship.

Mathew grinned.

“Welcome to the junkyard.”

Ryan smiled.

And together, they stepped outside.

The cockpit was suddenly quiet.

The seats were empty.

Outside the wide front window, the junkyard stretched across the dusty landscape like a mountain range made of broken machines.

Cranes creaked.

Metal clanged.

The giant pile of scrap metal stood like a rusty mountain, and the excavator slowly lifted another old car and dropped it onto the heap with a loud **CLANG**.

Inside the ship, the control panels blinked softly.

The engines ticked quietly as they cooled.

Everyone had stepped outside.

Down below, Uncle Ryan and the kids were walking across the junkyard floor toward Gavin.

From inside the empty cockpit, the ship seemed to watch silently over the endless fields of broken machines.

A small breeze blew dust across the ground.

Somewhere out there, among the piles of forgotten technology, thousands of strange machines waited to be discovered.

And today.

Four explorers had just arrived to start looking.

CHAPTER 13

The Junkyard

The junkyard was enormous.

Mountains of rusted machines rose like crooked hills. Old buses leaned against piles of twisted metal, and broken vehicles lay half-buried under years of discarded parts.

In the middle of the clearing, an excavator lifted another crushed car and dropped it onto the scrap pile.

CLANG.

But something else caught Uncle Ryan's eye.

Near the rusted bus, sitting quietly among the debris, was an old robot.

Its metal armor was covered in rust. One arm hung loosely, and wires trailed from its side. It looked like it had been sitting there for a very long time.

Mathew pointed.

"Uncle Ryan… look!"

Sybil leaned closer.

"Is it broken?"

Jacob studied it carefully.

"It looks… old."

Ryan walked closer and knelt beside the machine.

"This one is very old," he said softly.

He brushed some dust off the robot's shoulder plate.

"Probably from the early space wars."

Mathew's eyes widened.

"Can you fix it?"

Ryan smiled.

"That's the idea."

He tapped the robot lightly with his knuckles.

"Sometimes the oldest machines are the most interesting."

Behind them, the giant junkyard stretched out into the distance, full of forgotten technology and hidden stories.

And somewhere among all that scrap, many more machines were waiting to be found.

The three children carefully climbed down from the ship and walked across the dusty ground.

Pieces of old machines crunched under their shoes.

Ahead of them sat the rusty robot.

It didn't move.

It didn't make a sound.

Jacob folded his arms and studied it.

"It looks completely broken."

Sybil stepped a little closer.

"I feel a bit sorry for it."

Mathew leaned forward, staring at its glowing eye lens.

"Maybe it's just… sleeping."

The robot sat slumped against a pile of scrap metal, its body covered in rust and dents from battles long ago.

Old wires hung from its arm, and one of its legs looked badly damaged.

Jacob poked a loose piece of metal with his shoe.

"Why would anyone leave something like this here?"

Just then, Uncle Ryan's voice called from behind them.

"Because sometimes," he said, walking up beside them, "machines outlive their purpose."

He knelt down beside the robot and gently wiped dust from its chest plate.

A faint symbol appeared beneath the rust.

Ryan's eyes widened slightly.

"Well now… that's interesting."

Sybil tilted her head.

"What is it?"

Ryan smiled a little.

"This wasn't just any robot."

He tapped the metal lightly.

"This was once a **guardian unit**."

Mathew's eyes went wide.

"A guardian?!"

Ryan nodded.

“Long ago, machines like this protected entire colonies.”

Jacob studied the damaged joints, “Its actuator is broken.”

Sybil examined the symbol on its chest.
“That’s not a normal model.”

Mathew whispered,
“I think it’s lonely.”

It didn’t look like a hero anymore.

Just a tired old machine sitting in a junkyard.

Sybil whispered softly.

“Do you think it still works?”

Ryan looked at the robot thoughtfully.

Then he reached into his pocket and pulled out a small tool.

“There’s only one way to find out……………..No.”

CHAPTER 14

Meeting Gavin

The children stood quietly as Uncle Ryan walked over to the old man.

The junkyard manager leaned on his walking stick and smiled beneath his grey beard.

"Well now," he said, looking at the group, "not many visitors come wandering this far into the yard."

Ryan shook his hand.

"Gavin, good to see you, old friend."

The old man nodded.

"That's me. Keeper of broken machines and rusty secrets."

Behind them, the excavator slowly lifted another old car into the air.

Sybil pointed toward the rusty robot sitting near the bus.

"We saw that robot over there."

Gavin glanced at it and chuckled softly.

"Ah… that old thing."

Jacob frowned.

"Is it dangerous?"

Gavin shook his head.

"Not anymore."

He walked slowly toward the robot, tapping the ground with his stick.

"That one's been sitting there longer than I have."

Mathew's eyes widened.

"Really?"

Gavin nodded.

"Found it half-buried in the scrap pile many years ago. Never moved. Never powered on."

Ryan looked at the machine carefully.

"Looks like an old guardian unit."

Gavin raised an eyebrow.

"You know your machines."

Ryan smiled.

"A little."

The children gathered closer as Ryan crouched beside the robot again.

He brushed away more rust from its chest plate.

The symbol became clearer.

Ryan's expression changed.

"Huh."

Gavin noticed.

"What is it?"

Ryan looked up.

"This isn't just a guardian unit."

The children leaned in.

"What is it?" Sybil asked.

Ryan tapped the symbol again.

"This is a **prototype guardian**."

Gavin whistled softly.

"Well, I'll be…"

Jacob blinked.

“Is that important?”

Ryan nodded slowly.

“Very.”

He looked back at the silent robot.

“If this thing ever wakes up…”

Mathew whispered.

“…what would it do?”

Ryan smiled slightly.

“Protect something.”

The children looked at each other.

Then they all looked back at the old machine sitting quietly in the dust.

And for just a moment. Its eye flickered.

CHAPTER 15

The Request for Help

Ryan froze.

One of the fighting robots from before approached him.

It stood upright in front of him, tall and graceful, its white armor still scratched and dusty from years in the junkyard. Tiny lights flickered softly beneath its panels.

Its green eyes looked directly at him.

The robot's eyes flickered.

Its head turned slowly toward Ryan.

Then a quiet voice spoke:

"Ryan, could you help me?"

Ryan blinked twice.

"You… know my name?"

The robot tilted its head slightly, as if remembering something long forgotten.

"My memory banks are damaged," she said softly. "But your identity matches archived records."

Ryan looked stunned.

"Archived… records?"

Behind him, the children whispered excitedly.

"Did the robot just talk?" Mathew whispered.

Sybil's eyes were wide.

"She's beautiful…"

Jacob crossed his arms but couldn't hide his curiosity.

"Yeah… but how does she know Uncle Ryan?"

The robot's systems hummed quietly as faint lights pulsed through the cables in her neck.

"I was once assigned to assist engineers… long ago," she explained.

Ryan slowly stepped closer, studying the damaged panels on her arm.

"You've been here a very long time," he said gently.

"Yes," she replied.

A small spark flickered from a damaged joint.

“My systems are failing.”

She extended her hand slightly.

“Will you help me?”

Ryan smiled.

Behind him, the children cheered.

“Yes!” said Mathew.

“Can we help?” Sybil asked.

Ryan nodded.

“Looks like we’ve got ourselves a repair project.”

The robot looked at the group of smiling children.

For the first time in many years.

Her systems registered something new.

Spare Parts.

CHAPTER 16

Helping

Anistatica looked down at the children standing beside Ryan.

For a moment, she didn't answer.

Small lights flickered across the cables along her neck as damaged systems tried to restart.

Then she spoke softly.

"I was designed to assist engineers… and protect them."

Jacob raised an eyebrow.

"Protect them from what?"

Anistatica turned her head slowly toward the junkyard.

Her eyes scanned the mountains of scrap metal, the rusted ships, and the broken machines scattered across the valley.

"Danger," she replied.

Mathew looked around nervously.

"Danger. Like the fight you were in?"

Anistatica nodded.

"My sensors detected a Nanobot swarm unit."

Sybil tilted her head.

"The blue one?"

"Yes," Anistatica said.

"That unit is not supposed to be here."

Ryan frowned slightly.

"What do you mean?"

Anistatica's eyes dimmed briefly as she searched her damaged memory banks.

"That model was designed for dismantling hostile machines."

Jacob crossed his arms.

"So… it's basically a robot that eats other robots."

"Correct."

Mathew gulped.

"That sounds bad."

Ryan looked back toward the distant scrap piles where the blue Nanobot machine had disappeared.

"And you've been fighting it?"

"Yes," Anistatica said quietly.

"For a very long time."

Sybil stepped closer.

"Why?"

The android paused.

Then she answered with a calm certainty.

"Because it is hunting something."

Ryan looked surprised.

"Hunting what?"

Anistatica's green eyes turned toward the children.

"You."

The wind moved slowly across the junkyard.

Somewhere in the distance, metal shifted with a faint **CLANG**.

Ryan pushed his glasses up his nose.

"Well," he said slowly, "that definitely makes this repair project more interesting."

CHAPTER 17

The Good Deal

Ryan looked at the children and smiled.

"Well," he said, adjusting his glasses,
"That sounds like a pretty good deal."

Mathew's eyes lit up.

"A **Hammerhead Colonizer Spacecraft**?" he gasped.
"Is that a real spaceship?"

Anistatica nodded.

"Yes, a retired cargo hauler."

Jacob crossed his arms thoughtfully.

"Could it still fly?"

Anistatica's eyes flickered as she ran a diagnostic simulation.

"With repairs… yes."

Sybil clapped her hands excitedly.

"That would be amazing!"

Behind them, the small fluffy creature waddled forward.

It made a soft **"Floooz…"** sound.

Mathew turned and immediately crouched down.

"Whoa! Is that the **Fuzzy Floozag**?"

The creature blinked its huge eyes and wiggled happily.

"It's adorable!" Sybil said.

Ryan chuckled.

"Well, kids, looks like this junkyard has more surprises than we thought."

Anistatica tilted her head slightly.

"There are **many** things hidden here."

Ryan raised an eyebrow.

"Such as?"

Anistatica looked out across the endless mountains of scrap metal.

"Ancient machines… forgotten ships… and things that were never meant to be found again."

The children looked out across the vast junkyard.

Somewhere deep in the piles of rusted metal.

A faint metallic **CLANG… CLANG… CLANG…**

Echoed across the valley.

Jacob slowly looked back at Anistatica.

"…Was that supposed to happen?"

Anistatica's eyes glowed softly.

"No."

Ryan sighed.

"Well," he said, "Looks like our first repair job just found us."

Sybil bounced excitedly on her toes.

"I want to pat it! I want to pat the **Fuzzy Floozag**!"

The small creature blinked its huge sparkling eyes and waddled a little closer.

"Floooz…" it chirped happily.

Mathew laughed.

"I think it likes us!"

Jacob crouched down carefully.

“Wait,” he said cautiously. “What if it bites?”

Anistatica tilted her head slightly as her sensors scanned the fluffy creature.

“Fuzzy Floozags are harmless,” she said calmly.

“They are known for being friendly and… extremely affectionate.”

Sybil slowly reached out her hand.

The Floozag sniffed her fingers.

Then it leaned forward and gently **booped** her hand with its tiny nose.

Everyone burst out laughing.

“It’s so soft!” Sybil giggled.

Ryan smiled as he watched them.

“Well,” he said, “that might be the first happy thing to happen in this junkyard in a long time.”

But Anistatica was still looking out across the distant mountains of scrap metal.

Her eyes narrowed slightly.

"Ryan…"

Ryan glanced over.

"What is it?"

"My sensors detect movement."

The children froze.

"Movement?" Jacob asked.

"Where?"

Anistatica slowly raised her arm and pointed toward a dark ridge of broken machines.

"Over there."

From deep within the scrap pile.

Something large began to rise.

Metal shifted.

Rusty plates slid aside.

A massive silhouette slowly stood up from the junkyard.

Mathew whispered,

"Uh… Uncle Ryan…"

Ryan pushed his glasses up his nose.

"I'm guessing that's **not** the Hammerhead Colonizer."

Anistatica shook her head.

"No."

Her eyes glowed brighter.

"That is something much older."

Anistatica looked down at Ryan for a moment.

Small lights flickered across the panels along her arm as damaged systems tried to stabilize.

"I will try," she said quietly.

"But the Nanorobot is persistent."

Jacob frowned.

"What does that mean?"

Mathew swallowed nervously.

"And… what is its mission?"

Anistatica paused.

"Unknown."

Ryan cleared his throat and clapped his hands together.

"Well! That sounds like a problem for later."

He pointed back toward the distant ridge where a small metal building stood among piles of scrap.

"My workshop is over there."

Gavin nodded approvingly.

"Best repair shop in the junkyard," he said proudly.

"Mostly because it's the only one."

Sybil giggled.

The **Fuzzy Floozag** waddled after them as they started walking.

"Floooz… Floooz…"

Mathew laughed.

"I think it's coming with us!"

Anistatica suddenly stopped walking.

Her head tilted slightly.

Ryan noticed immediately.

"What is it?"

Her eyes glowed brighter.

"My sensors are detecting something."

Jacob looked around.

"Something like what?"

Anistatica slowly turned toward the distant mountains of scrap metal.

"Movement."

A deep metallic **THUD…**

Echoed across the junkyard.

Then another.

THUD… THUD…

Ryan sighed and adjusted his glasses.

"Please tell me that's not the Nanorobot again."

Anistatica's voice was calm.

"No."

She pointed toward the massive scrap piles.

“That… is much bigger.”

The children slowly turned to look.

From deep inside the rusted mountain of machines, a gigantic mechanical arm pushed scrap aside.

CHAPTER 18

The Strange House

The children stopped walking.

In front of them, sitting right in the middle of the giant junkyard, was the strangest house they had ever seen.

It looked old.

Very old.

The tall windows were dusty. The roof had strange antennas protruding from it. One side of the building leaned slightly, as if it had been pushed by something enormous.

But the strangest part was where the house stood.

Mountains of broken machines surrounded it.

Rusty engines.

Crushed vehicles.

Giant pieces of old spacecraft.

And in the middle of all that scrap sat Gavin's house.

Mathew stared with wide eyes.

"Wait… you live **here**?"

Gavin tapped his walking stick on the ground.

"Best view in the junkyard," he said proudly.

Jacob looked around at the piles of twisted metal.

"You call this a view?"

Gavin grinned.

"Every one of those piles is a story."

Sybil tilted her head and studied the house.

"Why does it have antennas on the roof?"

Gavin winked.

"Because this old place listens."

Ryan raised an eyebrow.

"Still collecting signals, Gavin?"

Gavin nodded.

"From ships."

"From satellites."

"Sometimes from things that aren't supposed to be talking anymore."

Mathew looked nervous.

"You mean… ghost ships?"

Gavin chuckled.

"Something like that."

Just then, the ground trembled slightly.

CLANG…

CLANG…

CLANG…

Ryan pushed his glasses up his nose and looked toward the distant scrap piles.

"Well," he said calmly.

"Looks like we might have visitors."

Anistatica's eyes glowed faint green.

Jacob swallowed.

Gavin slowly turned toward the mountains of scrap metal.

His smile faded just a little.

“Yes.”

He tapped his walking stick once more.

CHAPTER 19

The Junkyard Manager

The old man leaned on his walking stick and looked at the group carefully.

His sharp, grey eyes moved from Ryan.

To the children.

And finally, to the tall android standing beside them.

He raised one eyebrow.

“Well now,” he said slowly.

“That’s not something you see every day.”

Mathew stepped forward.

“Hi! Are you Gavin?”

The old man chuckled softly.

“That depends,” he said.

“Are you here to cause trouble?”

Sybil shook her head quickly.

"No, sir!"

Jacob folded his arms.

"We're just visiting."

Gavin nodded and tapped his walking stick on the ground.

"Good."

"Because this place has enough trouble already."

Ryan stepped forward and smiled.

"Kids, this is Gavin."

"The manager of the Intergalactic Junkyard."

Mathew's eyes widened.

"You run this whole place?"

Gavin scratched his beard.

"Someone has to keep the machines from wandering off."

The children looked confused.

Sybil tilted her head.

"Machines… wander?"

Gavin pointed his stick toward the distant scrap piles.

"In a place like this, old machines sometimes wake up."

Jacob looked interested.

"That sounds awesome."

Ryan sighed.

"It's usually less awesome than it sounds."

Gavin's eyes moved toward Anistatica again.

The android stood quietly beside them, her green optics glowing softly.

Gavin studied her carefully.

"Well now," he muttered.

"That's a Seeker unit."

Ryan nodded.

"Prototype model."

Gavin whistled quietly.

"Those were rare even before the space wars."

Mathew looked between them.

“So… she’s special?”

Gavin nodded slowly.

“Very.”

Anistatica stepped forward slightly.

“My systems are damaged,” she said calmly.

Ryan has agreed to help repair me.”

Gavin gave Ryan a long look.

“Of course he did.”

Ryan shrugged.

“I like a challenge.”

Gavin tapped his walking stick again and turned toward the strange house behind him.

“Well then,” he said.

“You’d better come inside.”

The children looked up at the tall, crooked house sitting in the middle of the junkyard.

Antennas pointed into the sky.

Strange wires ran along the roof.

And one of the windows flickered with dim yellow light.

Mathew whispered,

"Do you really live in there?"

Gavin grinned.

"Best listening post in the galaxy."

Sybil looked curious.

"Listening to what?"

Gavin paused at the bottom of the steps and looked back at them.

"Everything."

He slowly pointed his stick toward the mountains of scrap metal behind them.

"Because sometimes the junkyard talks."

At that moment—

A deep metallic **THUD** echoed across the valley.

Everyone froze.

Gavin looked toward the distant scrap piles.

His smile faded slightly.

He tapped the ground with his stick.

Anistatica's eyes glowed brighter.

"My sensors confirm movement."

Jacob looked toward the scrap mountains.

"Big movement."

Mathew whispered,

"How big?"

Metal groaned.

Rusty plates shifted.

Something enormous stood up from the wreckage.

Gavin sighed.

"Well, now looks like the junkyard wants to say hello."

CHAPTER 20

Treasure in the Dirt

While Uncle Ryan and Anistatica spoke with Gavin near the house, the children wandered a little farther into the junkyard.

Everywhere they looked, there were pieces of old machines.

Tiny gears.

Broken sensors.

Strange metal tubes.

It was like the ground itself was made of robot parts.

Jacob crouched down and started digging through the dirt.

"Look at this!" he said excitedly.

He pulled out a small metal device with three tiny arms.

Sybil leaned closer, brushing dust away from another piece.

"I think this is a sensor," she said. "See the lens?"

Mathew dug happily with both hands.

“Maybe we’ll find a whole robot!”

Behind them, Gavin slowly walked closer, tapping the ground with his stick.

Tap… tap… tap…

He watched the children quietly as they sorted through the strange parts.

Jacob proudly held up the small device.

“Do you think Uncle Ryan could fix this?”

Gavin scratched his beard.

“Maybe,” he said.

“But that piece didn’t come from just any machine.”

Sybil looked curious.

“What do you mean?”

Gavin pointed at the small metal object in Jacob’s hand.

“That’s a navigation stabilizer.”

Jacob blinked.

"For what?"

Gavin looked toward the enormous scrap piles stretching across the valley.

"For something that flies very fast."

Mathew's eyes widened.

"A spaceship?"

Gavin nodded slowly.

"Not just any spaceship."

He leaned on his stick and looked down at the scattered parts around them.

"All those pieces came from the same wreck."

Sybil brushed more dirt away and uncovered another piece of metal.

"Where is the rest of it?"

Gavin's eyes moved toward the distant mountain of scrap.

"Buried."

Jacob grinned.

"Then we should dig it out!"

Gavin chuckled.

"That ship has been buried there for fifty years."

Mathew looked impressed.

"Wow."

But Sybil noticed something strange.

One of the small metal pieces in the dirt was glowing faintly.

"Uh, guys?"

The others leaned closer.

The tiny device began to hum.

A soft blue light flickered across its surface.

Jacob slowly looked up at Gavin, "Was it supposed to do that?"

Gavin frowned.

"No."

The little device suddenly **beeped**.

And somewhere deep in the junkyard…

Something answered.

A low metallic **THOOM** echoed through the scrap mountains.

Gavin's expression turned serious.

"Well now," he muttered.

CHAPTER 21

Repairs

Inside Gavin's strange house, Ryan had turned one of the dusty rooms into a temporary workshop.

Old diagrams covered the walls.

Strange machines sat on wooden tables.

Tools were scattered everywhere.

And in the middle of the room sat Anistatica.

Ryan leaned close, carefully adjusting a tiny connection inside her arm.

"Hold still," he said.

Anistatica tilted her head slightly.

"My movement systems are currently limited," she replied calmly.

"That makes things easier," Ryan said with a small smile.

Tiny lights flickered along the cables inside her arm as he tightened the connection.

Sybil watched closely from the doorway.

"What does that part do?"

Ryan glanced over.

"Energy routing."

He pointed with the small tool.

"If this connection fails, half her systems shut down."

Mathew looked impressed.

"So you're fixing her brain?"

Ryan chuckled.

"Not exactly."

He tapped the open panel in her arm.

"This is more like fixing nerves."

Jacob leaned against the workbench.

"So once you finish, she'll be fully working again?"

Ryan hesitated.

"Maybe."

Anistatica looked down at the exposed components in her arm.

"My memory banks remain partially damaged," she said quietly.

Ryan nodded.

"That might take longer to repair."

For a moment, the room was quiet except for the faint hum of her internal systems.

Then Anistatica spoke again.

"Ryan."

"Yes?"

"My sensors are detecting a signal."

Ryan stopped working.

"What kind of signal?"

Anistatica's green eyes flickered.

"Unknown."

Jacob straightened up.

"From the junkyard?"

Anistatica slowly turned her head toward the window.

"Yes."

Outside, beyond Gavin's strange house, the endless mountains of scrap metal stretched across the valley.

Somewhere out there, something moved.

The signal pulsed again.

Stronger this time.

Ryan slowly pushed his glasses up his nose.

"Well," he said quietly.

"That can't be good."

Anistatica's optics glowed brighter.

"It is coming closer."

From deep in the junkyard, a low metallic **THUD** echoed across the valley.

And then another.

THUD…

THUD…

Jacob looked toward the window.

"Uh… Uncle Ryan?"

Ryan sighed.

"I'm guessing the repair job just became urgent."

Anistatica's systems hummed softly.

"My combat protocols are still offline."

Ryan looked at the open panel in her arm.

"Then I'd better work faster."

Outside the house, something enormous was waking up.

CHAPTER 22

The Mud Field

The rain had turned part of the junkyard into a swamp.

Mathew stepped forward.

SPLAT.

His boot disappeared halfway into the mud.

He looked down and laughed.

“This place is amazing.”

Jacob rolled his eyes.

“It’s a junkyard.”

Mathew stomped again.

Mud splashed everywhere.

Sybil giggled.

“Careful!”

Too late.

Mathew slipped.

SPLOOSH.

Mud flew into the air.

Jacob burst out laughing.

Within seconds, all three kids were sliding and splashing through the thick brown sludge.

From the porch of the crooked house, Gavin watched them.

He smiled.

Kids almost never visited the junkyard.

Then his smile faded.

Far beyond the muddy field…

A pile of scrap metal moved.

The three children froze.

Jacob looked down at his muddy hands.

Sybil stared at the brown splashes on her shirt.

Mathew wiped his face… which only made things worse.

They all looked at each other.

Then they burst out laughing.

"It wasn't our fault!" Mathew said between giggles.

"There was a giant mud puddle!" Jacob added.

"And we were just investigating it!" Sybil said proudly.

Anistatica placed her hands on her hips.

Even with the mud splattered across her white armor, she still managed to look very serious.

"Investigations are not normally conducted by throwing mud," she said.

Jacob shrugged.

"It was scientific."

Sybil nodded enthusiastically.

"Very scientific."

Mathew held up a muddy bolt he had found.

"Look! We discovered this!"

Anistatica looked at the metal piece.

Her eyes flickered as she scanned it.

"Interesting."

Jacob blinked.

"Wait… really?"

Anistatica nodded.

"That component appears to be part of an early navigation unit."

Sybil's eyes widened.

"So we did discover something!"

Anistatica paused for a moment.

Then she pointed toward Gavin's strange house.

"Nevertheless, all three of you require cleaning."

Mathew groaned.

"Aww…"

Jacob sighed.

"Worth it."

Sybil looked at her muddy hands again and giggled.

"Totally worth it."

Behind them, the crooked house stood quietly in the middle of the endless junkyard.

But far beyond the muddy field, the mountains of scrap metal shifted again.

A faint metallic rumble rolled across the valley.

Anistatica turned her head slowly toward the sound.

Her sensors flickered.

Something large… was still moving out there.

And it was getting closer.

CHAPTER 23

Incoming

Anistatica suddenly froze.

All the small lights across her body turned bright red.

Her eyes glowed like warning beacons.

"Danger," she announced.

"I detect an incoming spacecraft crash. Please relocate to safety."

The children stopped laughing.

Jacob looked up at the sky.

"Wait… what?"

Sybil pushed her muddy glasses back onto her nose.

"A crash?"

Mathew squinted upward.

"I don't see anything."

Behind them, Gavin shaded his eyes with one hand and stared toward the clouds.

"Oh," he muttered.

"I think that might be a big one."

At first, the sky looked normal.

Grey clouds drifted slowly above the endless junkyard.

Then—

A tiny streak of light appeared far above them.

It grew brighter.

And brighter.

And brighter.

The streak turned into a blazing line of fire ripping through the clouds.

Mathew's mouth dropped open.

"Whoa."

Sybil pointed upward.

"It's coming straight down!"

The sound arrived a moment later.

A deep roaring scream of engines and tearing metal.

The ground trembled beneath their feet.

Anistatica stepped forward immediately, placing herself between the children and the sky.

"Impact predicted in thirty seconds."

Jacob swallowed.

"Thirty seconds?!"

Gavin tapped his stick hard against the ground.

"Inside the house!" he shouted.

"Now!"

But the fiery spacecraft was already tearing through the clouds.

And it was coming directly toward the junkyard.

CHAPTER 24

The Sky Breaks

The burning spacecraft tore through the clouds like a blazing comet.

Flames streaked across the sky in long, glowing trails.

Metal plates ripped away from the hull and tumbled through the air.

Everyone in the junkyard stared upward.

For a moment, no one moved.

The ship was enormous.

Much bigger than the little salvage craft that usually crashed here.

Anistatica's warning lights pulsed brighter.

"Impact imminent," she announced.

"Estimated collision in twelve seconds."

Mathew grabbed Jacob's arm.

"Is it going to hit us?!"

Jacob shook his head nervously.

“I… I don’t know!”

Sybil stared wide-eyed as pieces of the spacecraft broke away and whistled toward the junkyard.

“It’s falling apart!”

Ryan stepped forward quickly.

“Everyone back!”

Gavin tapped his walking stick hard against the ground.

“Inside the house!” he shouted.

But the sky above them suddenly exploded with light.

A massive section of the hull sheared away, spinning through the air like a flaming blade.

Chunks of burning metal rained down across the junkyard.

Anistatica moved instantly.

She stepped in front of the children and raised both arms.

BOOM!

The ground shook violently.

Dust and sparks blasted into the air.

Mathew covered his ears.

“That was huge!”

Jacob pointed upward.

Gavin squinted at the flaming wreckage.

Then he muttered quietly,

“Well, now that’s going to make quite a mess.”

The burning hull slammed into the junkyard with a thunderous crash.

The entire valley shook.

Mountains of scrap metal collapsed.

Dust rose into the sky like a giant storm cloud.

CHAPTER 25

The Fire Cloud

The crashing spacecraft finally hit the junkyard.

For one silent second…

Nothing happened.

Then the world exploded.

A blinding flash lit up the valley.

A gigantic fireball erupted from the mountains of scrap metal, rising higher and higher into the sky.

BOOOOM!

The ground shook so hard that the children nearly fell over.

A massive cloud of fire and smoke climbed upward, spreading into a giant glowing mushroom shape above the junkyard.

Mathew's mouth hung open.

"Whoa…"

Sybil stared at the enormous cloud.

"I've never seen anything like that!"

Jacob slowly lowered his hand from shielding his eyes.

"That ship… completely exploded."

Anistatica's warning lights continued flashing red across her armor.

"Warning," she said calmly.

"High levels of heat, radiation, and falling debris detected."

Burning pieces of metal began raining down across the junkyard.

Some crashed into distant piles of scrap.

Others skidded across the muddy ground nearby.

Gavin stood quietly beside his house, leaning on his stick.

He watched the towering fire cloud with a thoughtful expression.

"Well now," he muttered.

"That's definitely one of the bigger ones."

Ryan stepped outside the house and looked toward the explosion.

He pushed his glasses up his nose.

“Everyone okay?”

The children nodded.

“We’re fine!” Mathew shouted.

Anistatica turned her head toward the distant crash site.

Her sensors scanned the burning wreckage.

“Multiple structural fragments detected,” she reported.

“However…”

She paused.

Ryan frowned.

“However, what?”

Anistatica’s glowing eyes narrowed slightly.

“There appears to be movement inside the debris field.”

Jacob blinked.

"Movement?"

Sybil swallowed nervously.

"You mean… something survived that?"

Anistatica looked toward the burning scrap piles in the distance.

"Yes."

A faint metallic shape slowly began to rise from the flaming wreckage.

And whatever had just climbed out of that destroyed spacecraft was still alive.

CHAPTER 26

Clean Up

Inside Gavin's house, things were much calmer.

The old building smelled like warm tea, machine oil, and dusty books.

The children sat on wooden stools while Ryan and Anistatica tried to clean them up.

It wasn't easy.

Mud was everywhere.

On their clothes.

In their hair.

Even behind their ears.

Jacob laughed as Ryan rubbed his hair with a towel.

"Hey! That tickles!"

Sybil peeked out from under a large towel that Anistatica had gently wrapped around her head.

"I think I'm cleaner already," she said proudly.

Mathew sat nearby, wrapped up like a burrito in another towel.

"I look like a muddy ghost," he giggled.

Anistatica carefully brushed some dirt from Sybil's glasses.

Her movements were gentle and precise.

"Cleaning progress: seventy-two percent," she announced.

Gavin watched from across the room, smiling as he sipped from a small metal cup.

"Well now," he said.

"You lot look a bit more like explorers and a bit less like swamp creatures."

Mathew laughed.

"Hey! We discovered important junk!"

Ryan chuckled.

"That's how science usually starts."

For a moment, everything felt warm and peaceful inside the old house.

The fire crackled softly in the stove.

The storm of dust outside slowly settled.

But then Anistatica suddenly stopped moving.

The small lights along her neck flickered.

Her eyes focused toward the window.

Ryan noticed immediately.

"What is it?"

Anistatica's voice lowered slightly.

"My sensors are detecting movement near the crash site."

Jacob leaned forward.

"You mean the ship that exploded?"

"Yes," she replied.

Her eyes glowed faintly.

"Something has emerged from the wreckage."

Outside the crooked house, the glowing fire cloud still burned in the distance.

And whatever had climbed out of the destroyed spacecraft was now moving toward the junkyard.

Inside Gavin's house, the mood had changed completely.

The muddy chaos from earlier had turned into a full clean-up operation.

Buckets of warm water sat on the floor.

Towels were piled everywhere.

Soap bubbles floated through the air.

Jacob rubbed his hair with a towel while Ryan tried to wipe a stubborn patch of mud from his cheek.

"Hold still," Ryan said.

Nearby, Sybil sat wrapped in a large towel like a tiny scientist after an experiment.

Mathew sat beside her, still laughing as Gavin poured warm water into the wash basin.

Anistatica carefully wiped the last bits of mud from Sybil's glasses.

"Cleaning process ninety-three percent complete," she announced.

Sybil grinned.

"That's a good score!"

Suddenly, Mathew pointed excitedly.

"I want to pat the **Fuzzy Floozag!**"

Everyone looked down.

Sitting happily in the middle of the room was a small purple creature covered in soft, fuzzy fur.

It had huge shiny eyes, tiny curling tentacles, and a long fluffy tail that wagged like a happy puppy.

"Floooz…" the creature chirped.

Jacob leaned forward.

"Where did that thing come from?"

Gavin chuckled and stroked his beard.

"That little fellow wandered in during the explosion."

Sybil's eyes sparkled.

"It's adorable!"

The Floozag bounced happily in Mathew's lap and made another cheerful sound.

"Floooz floooz!"

Ryan laughed.

"Well, at least something good came out of that crash."

But at that exact moment..

Anistatica's eyes flickered.

A faint red light returned behind her pupils.

She slowly turned her head toward the window.

Outside, the fiery glow of the distant crash still burned across the sky.

Her voice became quiet and serious again.

"My sensors are detecting movement approaching the house."

Jacob blinked.

"Movement?"

Anistatica nodded.

"Yes."

She paused.

"It appears…"

"…we are about to receive a visitor."

CHAPTER 27

Something Big

The room had finally begun to feel calm again.

The children were wrapped in clean towels.

The muddy water had been poured out.

The Fuzzy Floozag sat happily on the wooden chair, blinking its enormous, shiny eyes.

"Floooz…" it chirped softly.

Mathew giggled.

"I think it likes us."

Sybil nodded.

"It definitely likes you."

Jacob leaned forward and scratched the creature gently behind one of its fuzzy antennae.

The Floozag purred.

Ryan smiled.

"Well, that's a good sign."

But Anistatica was still looking toward the window.

Her sensors continued scanning the junkyard outside.

After a moment, she turned back toward the group.

"Well, okay," she said calmly.

"If Ryan says it is okay, follow me."

The children looked up at her.

"Follow you where?" Jacob asked.

Anistatica pointed toward the door that led outside.

"She is rather large."

Sybil blinked.

"She?"

Mathew's eyes widened.

"You mean… the thing from the crash?"

Anistatica nodded.

"Yes."

Ryan raised an eyebrow.

"You're sure it's not hostile?"

Anistatica paused for a moment while her systems analyzed the readings.

"No immediate threat detected."

Gavin leaned on his walking stick and chuckled.

"Well now," he said.

"That's something you don't hear every day."

The Floozag bounced excitedly on the chair.

"Floooz!"

Jacob looked at the others.

"So…"

"…we're going outside to meet a giant alien that just crashed out of the sky?"

Ryan shrugged.

"Looks like it."

Anistatica opened the creaky wooden door.

Outside, the distant wreckage still glowed across the junkyard.

And somewhere out there. Something very large was waiting for them.

CHAPTER 28

The Giant Floozag

The group walked slowly across the junkyard.

Broken machines and twisted metal lay everywhere from the massive explosion.

The air still smelled like smoke.

Anistatica led the way.

Her sensors quietly scanned the wreckage as the children followed behind her in their oversized towels.

Jacob whispered, "So… how big did you say it was?"

Anistatica replied calmly.

"Rather large."

They turned around a tall pile of scrap metal.

And then they saw it.

Mathew stopped walking.

"Whoa…"

In the middle of the junkyard sat a giant metal cage.

And inside the cage was the biggest creature any of them had ever seen.

It looked like the tiny Floozag they had found in the house.

Except this one was enormous.

Its fuzzy purple body filled nearly the entire cage.

Huge, round eyes blinked slowly behind the metal bars.

Soft glowing antennae wiggled gently above its head.

“Flooooz…” it rumbled in a deep, friendly voice.

Sybil’s jaw dropped.

“That’s the mama Floozag!”

Jacob nodded slowly.

“It must be.”

The giant creature blinked at them with enormous, curious eyes.

Then it leaned forward slightly and sniffed the air.

"Flooooz flooooz…"

Mathew waved excitedly.

"Hi!"

The creature's fluffy antennae twitched happily.

Anistatica studied the cage carefully.

"This containment unit appears to have been part of the crashed spacecraft."

Ryan stepped closer and examined the heavy metal lock.

"So someone was transporting it."

Gavin tapped his walking stick against the ground.

"Well now," he said quietly.

"That explains the explosion."

Sybil looked up at Ryan.

"Are we going to let it out?"

Ryan looked at the giant fuzzy creature.

The creature blinked slowly back at him.

Then it made a soft, hopeful sound.

"Floooz…"

Ryan sighed.

"I have a feeling that cage isn't going to hold her for very long."

CHAPTER 29

Hello, Big Floozag

The giant Floozag leaned closer to the bars of the cage.

Its enormous eyes shimmered like tiny galaxies.

Jacob slowly raised his hand and pressed it gently against the cold metal bars.

“Hi there,” he said softly.

Mathew copied him and reached up too.

Sybil leaned forward beside them.

The creature blinked slowly.

Then it moved its huge fuzzy face closer until its nose nearly touched the bars.

“Flooooz…” it hummed.

Its voice was deep and warm, like a giant purring engine.

The children giggled.

“I think it likes us!” Mathew said.

Jacob nodded.

“It definitely does.”

The Floozag lifted one enormous fuzzy paw and gently pressed it against the bars where their hands were.

Even through the cage, they could feel the warmth of its fur.

Behind them, Anistatica watched carefully.

Her sensors scanned the creature from head to toe.

“No signs of aggression,” she reported.

Ryan walked around the side of the cage, examining the heavy metal hinges.

“Whatever ship was carrying this,” he said, “they built this cage to be strong.”

Gavin tapped the cage bars with his walking stick.

CLANG.

“Well now,” he said.

“If that big fluffball decides to lean on it, I don’t think these bars will last long.”

The Floozag blinked again and made a soft, happy sound.

"Floooz floooz…"

Sybil turned to Ryan.

"Can we let her out?"

Ryan rubbed his chin thoughtfully.

"That depends."

He pointed toward the giant creature.

"We need to know one thing first."

Jacob looked up.

"What?"

Ryan smiled slightly.

"Whether she's friendly…"

The Floozag tilted its head.

Then it suddenly licked the cage bars with a huge fuzzy tongue.

The children burst out laughing, "or just very hungry."

CHAPTER 30

The Keeper

The giant Floozag blinked slowly inside the cage.

“Flooooz…”

Suddenly—

Blue sparks flashed in the air.

The children jumped.

A tall silver figure appeared beside the cage.

Her body shimmered like polished chrome.

Floating machines orbited her waist like silent satellites.

Jacob whispered,

“Whoa…”

The robot turned calmly toward them.

Her voice was smooth and cold.

Sybil stepped closer.

She placed one hand on the cage.

"This creature belongs to me."

Anistatica stepped forward immediately.

"Nanobot."

The silver robot smiled slightly.

"So we meet again."

Ryan pushed his glasses up his nose.

"Well," he muttered.

"That can't be good."

CHAPTER 31

Old Promises

The wind across the junkyard grew colder.

Loose pieces of metal rattled softly in the distance.

Anistatica stepped forward, pointing directly at the shining silver woman.

"Nanobot," she said firmly.

"I have promised **not** to fight you."

The children looked back and forth between the two robots.

Jacob whispered, "Wait… they know each other?"

Sybil nodded slowly.

"I think they do."

The silver Nanobot lowered her visor slightly and smiled.

"Yes," she said calmly.

Blue sparks flickered around the strange floating device beside her hand.

The machine hummed quietly as if ready to activate.

The giant Floozag blinked inside the cage.

"Flooooz…"

Mathew gently patted the bars again.

"It's okay," he whispered.

Gavin leaned on his walking stick and chuckled.

"Well now," he said.

"This junkyard is getting more interesting every minute."

Nanobot turned toward the distant scrap mountains.

Her smile faded.

Anistatica's sensors lit up again.

Pieces of broken spacecraft.

Ryan stared in disbelief.

The wind across the junkyard fell silent.

Even the giant Floozag stopped moving inside the cage.

The silver robot slowly lifted her head.

Blue electricity crackled around the strange device floating beside her.

“I don’t care,” she said coldly.

“I will destroy you.”

The children froze.

Mathew looked up nervously at Ryan.

“Uh… that sounds bad.”

Sybil whispered, “Very bad.”

Jacob slowly stepped back from the cage.

Anistatica didn’t move.

Her eyes glowed steadily as she pointed toward the silver figure.

The Nanobots visor flickered with lines of data.

Ryan frowned.

Gavin leaned on his stick and muttered,

“Well now… that doesn’t sound ideal.”

Behind them, the giant Floozag made a soft, worried sound.

“Floooz…”

The children looked back at the creature.

Its huge eyes blinked slowly, filled with gentle confusion.

It clearly had no idea why everyone was suddenly so tense.

Anistatica lowered her arm slightly.

The Nanobot looked toward the horizon.

Far across the junkyard, the scrap mountains began shifting again.

Pieces of metal slowly lifted into the air.

They twisted together like a storm made of machines.

Ryan exhaled slowly.

“Well,” he said.

“I guess we’re about to find out just how strong a junkyard can be.”

CHAPTER 32

The Floozag's Choice

The sky above the junkyard burned orange as the sun dropped behind the scrap mountains.

Anistatica stood perfectly still.

Across from her, the silver Nanobot shimmered like liquid metal. Tiny sparks of blue energy danced around the strange floating device beside her hand.

The children watched nervously.

Jacob whispered,
"Please tell me they're not about to fight again."

Sybil pushed her glasses up.

"I think they are."

Nanobot's visor flickered with streams of data.

"You should not have repaired the Seeker unit," she said coldly.

Anistatica raised one hand calmly.

"I gave my word. I will not fight you."

Nanobot smiled.

"That promise only applied to you."

Blue electricity crackled around the floating device.

The scrap metal across the junkyard began to tremble.

Mathew swallowed.

"That looks… bad."

Ryan sighed and rubbed his forehead.

"Yep. Definitely bad."

Behind them, the giant Floozag pressed her enormous nose against the bars of the cage.

"Flooooz?"

She watched the rising storm of metal.

The Nanobot lifted her arm.

Thousands of tiny machines poured from the floating device like a cloud of glittering dust.

The swarm rose into the air.

Pieces of junk lifted off the ground.

Engines.

Bolts.

Broken panels.

All of it spiraling into a growing storm of metal.

Jacob stepped back.

"That thing is building something."

Sybil nodded slowly.

"A giant robot."

Ryan pushed his glasses up his nose.

"Well… that's inconvenient."

Suddenly—

The giant Floozag lost patience.

"FLOOOOZ!"

With a deep rumbling growl, she wrapped one enormous fuzzy paw around the cage bars.

The metal bent instantly.

CLANG.

The bars snapped.

The cage door ripped open.

Before anyone could react,

The Floozag reached forward and grabbed the Nanobot.

CRUNCH.

Metal shattered.

Blue sparks exploded as the Nanobot broke into pieces.

Bolts clattered across the junkyard floor.

The children stared in amazement.

Mathew gasped.

“She just… squished her!”

The Floozag blinked proudly.

“Flooooz.”

Ryan nodded thoughtfully.

“Well.”

“That answers one question.”

Gavin leaned on his stick and chuckled.

"Indeed, it does."

But far across the junkyard, the storm of metal was still growing.

Because the Nanobot swarm was still alive.

And it was rebuilding.

CHAPTER 33

Awakening the Machine

Ryan knelt beside the rust-covered maintenance robot.

“Let’s see what we’ve got here.”

He pried open a cracked metal panel.

Inside, tangled wires glowed faint green.

Jacob leaned closer.

“That thing looks ancient.”

Ryan grinned.

“Ancient machines are the best kind.”

He connected two wires.

SPARK.

The robot shuddered.

Sybil gasped.

“It moved!”

Anistatica scanned the machine.

“Power systems reactivating.”

Ryan wiped rust from a small circular core buried deep inside the robot’s chest.

The green light pulsed brighter.

WHRRRRR…

Gears began turning.

Panels unfolded.

Tiny robotic arms clicked into place.

Jacob’s eyes widened.

“It’s transforming!”

Ryan laughed.

“That’s the self-repair system.”

With a loud CLUNK, the cracked shell opened.

A transparent dome rose slowly from the center of the machine.

Inside it, the glowing green processor floated like a tiny planet.

A mechanical voice echoed from the robot.

"Maintenance unit restored."

"Searching for Hammerhead-class vessel."

Ryan pushed his glasses up his nose.

"Perfect."

The green light pulsed again.

High above the planet—

Something answered.

The ground vibrated slightly.

Mathew looked up.

"Did you feel that?"

Ryan grinned.

"Oh yes."

"That means the Hammerhead just woke up."

CHAPTER 34

Follow that Maintenance Robot

The maintenance robot suddenly roared to life.

Jets of bright flame blasted from its underside as the newly repaired engines ignited.

Jacob gasped and grabbed his coat.

"It's taking off!"

The small craft lifted from the pile of scrap metal, shaking loose rust and debris as it rose into the darkening sky.

Anistatica watched calmly, her glowing sensors tracking its trajectory.

"Maintenance unit returning to orbital vessel," she said.

Ryan shaded his eyes and grinned up at the rising rocket.

"Perfect," he said.

"That means the Hammerhead's repair system just got its mechanic back."

The rocket streaked upward, leaving a glowing trail of fire behind it as it climbed toward the stars.

Jacob stared, wide-eyed.

"So… what happens now?"

Ryan chuckled.

"Now the Hammerhead wakes up."

High above the planet, far beyond the clouds, the maintenance robot sped toward the enormous cargo ship, silently orbiting.

Deep within the ship's ancient systems, dormant circuits flickered.

Lights began turning on.

Engines slowly warmed.

And across the entire Intergalactic Junkyard.

The sky started to glow.

Ryan didn't wait for anyone to answer.

He was already running.

His muddy lab coat flapped wildly behind him as he sprinted across the uneven piles of scrap metal.

"Come on!" he shouted. "We don't have much time!"

Jacob scrambled after him, nearly tripping over a rusted gear.

"Wait—catch *what*?" he yelled.

Ryan pointed toward the glowing sky where the maintenance robot had disappeared.

"The Hammerhead!"

Sybil ran beside Anistatica, pushing her glasses up as she tried to keep up.

"You mean the ship is actually waking up?"

Anistatica's sensors flickered as she scanned the sky.

"Orbital vessel engines are powering online," she confirmed.

Mathew's eyes widened.

"So it's coming down here?!"

Ryan laughed breathlessly as he ran.

"Not exactly!"

Ahead of them, the red shuttle Lost Rider sat, its cargo ramp glowing with warm yellow light.

"If we launch now," Ryan said, "we can intercept it before it leaves orbit!"

Jacob's jaw dropped.

"You want to chase a spaceship…?"

Ryan skidded to a stop at the bottom of the shuttle ramp and turned with a huge grin.

"Of course!"

Behind them, the sky shimmered as distant engines ignited far above the planet.

Ryan pointed dramatically at the open shuttle door.

"Everyone aboard!"

Because the race to catch the Hammerhead… had just begun.

CHAPTER 35

Away They Go

The shuttle doors slammed shut with a loud **CLANG**.

Ryan dropped into the pilot's seat and strapped himself in.

"Everyone buckled up?" he asked cheerfully.

Jacob was already gripping the control stick.

"I've got navigation!" he said confidently.

Sybil leaned forward in her seat, staring out at the endless stars through the cockpit window.

"It's beautiful…" she whispered.

Mathew bounced excitedly.

"Are we really chasing a spaceship?!"

Ryan pushed his glasses up his nose and flipped several glowing switches.

"Not just any spaceship," he said.

"The Hammerhead."

Behind them, Anistatica calmly connected a cable from her arm into the shuttle's control console.

"Shuttle systems synchronized," she reported.

"Trajectory toward Hammerhead orbital vector calculated."

Jacob frowned slightly as he studied the instruments.

"Uh… Uncle Ryan?"

Ryan looked over.

"Yes?"

Jacob pointed at the radar screen.

The cockpit grew quiet.

Ryan leaned forward and looked at the display.

A second signal blinked beside the Hammerhead's icon.

Sybil tilted her head.

"What is that?"

Anistatica's eyes glowed brighter as she analyzed the data.

"Another broken maintenance robot being repaired by the first," she said.

Mathew gulped.

Ryan slowly smiled.

"Well," he said.

"Looks like the race just got interesting."

Outside the shuttle window, the stars stretched ahead as their small craft accelerated into the darkness of space.

Far below the stars, their ship streaked through the sky.

It was sleek, bright red, and incredibly fast.

Twin engines burned blue as the craft cut through the upper atmosphere like a blade.

Painted boldly on the side were the words:

LAST RIDER

Inside the cockpit, a Ryan leaned forward with a confident grin.

Ryan tapped a glowing control panel.

"Target confirmed."

On the radar screen ahead, two signals blinked.

One was small, the shuttle Uncle Ryan and the kids had just launched.

The other was enormous.

The **Hammerhead**.

Uncle Ryan chuckled.

“Well, well, looks like that ship is mine.”

The Last Rider’s engines roared louder.

The red craft accelerated, climbing higher toward orbit.

Uncle Ryan’s little shuttle was already racing toward the stars.

And the chase for the Hammerhead had just become a race.

CHAPTER 36

The Hammerhead

Ryan leaned forward in his seat, pointing excitedly through the wide cockpit window.

"There it is!"

Far ahead, a small craft streaked across the stars, leaving a brilliant blue trail behind it.

Jacob squinted at the radar screen.

"That's the maintenance robot!"

Sybil leaned closer to the window.

"And it's heading straight for the Hammerhead."

Mathew bounced in his chair.

"Are we going to catch it?!"

Ryan grabbed the throttle and pushed it forward.

The shuttle engines roared.

"We're certainly going to try!"

Anistatica calmly studied the navigation display.

“Intercept trajectory calculated,” she said.

Jacob looked up.

Anistatica nodded.

“Yes.”

Ryan’s grin widened.

“Better get there first.”

The shuttle surged forward through the stars, racing toward the distant maintenance robot and the enormous Hammerhead waiting in orbit.

The sleek red **Last Rider** was closing in fast.

Far above the planet, the **Hammerhead** drifted silently through orbit.

It was enormous.

The ancient cargo ship stretched across the stars like a floating city, its massive engines dark and silent after years of neglect.

But now, small lights were beginning to glow along its hull.

Deep inside the ship, systems that had slept for decades slowly flickered back to life.

The maintenance robot streaked toward the vessel, its engines blazing as it approached the giant docking bay.

A faint transmission echoed across space.

“Maintenance unit returning to Hammerhead.”

Inside the massive ship, dormant repair systems began to awaken.

Panels opened.

Mechanical arms unfolded.

Energy flowed through long-silent circuits.

Below, on the planet’s surface, the Intergalactic Junkyard stretched across the horizon like a metal ocean.

And racing toward the giant ship were two very different spacecraft.

One small and battered.

The other is sleek and red.

Inside Uncle Ryan’s shuttle, the crew watched the Hammerhead grow larger in the window.

Jacob whispered in awe.

"It's huge…"

Ryan smiled.

"Yep."

He gently pushed the shuttle's controls forward.

"And we're about to board it."

Closing fast through the stars, the **Last Rider** feathered its engines.

As the shuttle closed in, the **Hammerhead** began to change.

Panels along the giant ship's hull slid open with slow mechanical groans.

One by one, small spherical machines emerged from hidden ports.

Ryan leaned forward in his seat.

"Whoa…"

Jacob pointed at the window.

"Look!"

The maintenance robots swarmed across the massive hull like tiny metal spiders.

Bright green eyes glowed as they began welding and repairing the ancient ship.

Sparks burst across the Hammerhead's battered surface.

Sybil watched in amazement.

"They're fixing it!"

Anistatica nodded.

"Autonomous repair drones," she said.

"Standard Hammerhead maintenance protocol."

One drone sealed a massive crack in the engine housing.

Another replaced entire plates of damaged armor.

Dozens more crawled across the ship, their welding torches blazing like tiny stars.

Ryan smiled proudly.

"Now that's good engineering."

Jacob studied the radar screen again.

"Uh… Uncle Ryan?"

Ryan glanced over.

"Yes?"

Jacob pointed nervously.

Ryan looked back at the enormous ship filling the window.

"Well," he said calmly.

"Then we'd better get aboard."

Ahead of them, the giant docking bay of the **Hammerhead** slowly began to open.

CHAPTER 37

It is Working

Ryan kept his finger pointed out the cockpit window as the massive ship filled their view.

The **Hammerhead** looked even bigger up close.

Repair drones buzzed around its hull like glowing fireflies, welding panels and sealing cracks.

Jacob tightened his grip on the controls.

“Docking bay ahead!” he said.

A huge circular opening slowly rotated open along the ship’s side.

Inside, rows of ancient lights flickered back to life.

Sybil leaned forward excitedly.

“It’s actually working!”

Anistatica studied the navigation screen.

“Docking corridor is stabilizing,” she said.

“Landing clearance granted by Hammerhead autonomous systems.”

Mathew pumped his fist.

“We did it!”

Ryan smiled and gently adjusted the shuttle’s thrusters.

“Alright, crew,” he said.

“Let’s bring her in.”

The shuttle glided toward the enormous docking bay.

Outside, the sleek red ship suddenly burst into view, streaking toward the docking bay.

Sybil gasped.

Ryan’s eyes sparkled with excitement.

“Well,” he said calmly.

He pushed the throttle forward.

The shuttle surged toward the Hammerhead’s docking bay as the red **Last Rider** closed in fast.

The sleek red **Last Rider** shot forward like a missile.

Its engines roared as the craft surged straight toward the open docking bay of the **Hammerhead**.

Inside Uncle Ryan's shuttle, the radar alarm began beeping rapidly.

Jacob's eyes widened.

"We are going in!"

Ryan leaned forward in his seat and squinted through the cockpit window.

Sure enough, the red ship was already sliding toward the glowing entrance of the giant cargo vessel.

Sybil gasped.

Mathew pointed excitedly.

"Look! We are docking!"

The **Last Rider** streaked into the docking bay, its engines blazing as it crossed the threshold of the massive ship.

Inside the Hammerhead, ancient docking lights flickered brighter as the vessel welcomed its first visitor in years.

Ryan rubbed his chin thoughtfully.

"Well… that's interesting."

Jacob looked worried.

Ryan grinned.

He gently pushed the shuttle controls forward.

“They just opened the door for us.”

The battered shuttle glided toward the massive docking bay, following the red ship inside the giant Hammerhead.

And somewhere deep inside the ancient cargo vessel, systems were waking up that no one had touched for centuries.

CHAPTER 38

A New Beginning

The shuttle glided gently into the massive docking bay of the Hammerhead.

The enormous cargo ship hummed softly around them.

Lights flickered across the ancient walls.

For the first time in decades, the ship was alive again.

Ryan powered down the engines.

“Well,” he said, stretching.

“That was exciting.”

Jacob climbed out of his seat.

“We fixed a spaceship.”

Sybil nodded.

“And saved a giant alien.”

Mathew held up the tiny repair drone he had been tinkering with.

"And we got a robot friend!"

Anistatica stood beside them, her sensors glowing calmly.

"All Hammerhead systems are stable," she reported.

"Navigation and life-support operational."

Ryan smiled.

"Then our job here is done."

Outside the docking bay window, the stars stretched endlessly across space.

Far below them, the planet of the Intergalactic Junkyard glittered with mountains of scrap metal.

Gavin's voice crackled over the radio.

"Ryan?"

Ryan tapped the communicator.

"Go ahead."

"You planning to bring that ship back down here?"

Ryan looked at the enormous Hammerhead around them.

Then he smiled.

"Eventually."

"But first…"

He turned to the kids.

"…how would you like to take the biggest cargo ship in the galaxy for a test flight?"

Mathew nearly exploded with excitement.

"YES!"

Jacob grinned.

Sybil adjusted her glasses.

"Best field trip ever."

Ryan pushed his glasses up his nose and sat back in the captain's chair.

"Alright, crew."

"Let's see what this old ship can do."

Outside the Hammerhead, its massive engines began to glow.

Slowly.

The giant cargo vessel turned toward the stars.

Because somewhere out there.

Another adventure was waiting.

The End.

www.ingramcontent.com/pod-product-compliance
Lightning Source LLC
LaVergne TN
LVHW010617100826
845148LV00014B/3009